M000304369

KAIJU APOCALYPSE III

ERIC S BROWN
JASON CORDOVA

Copyright © 2014 by Eric S Brown and Jason Cordova
Copyright © 2014 by Severed Press
www.severedpress.com
All rights reserved. No part of this book may be
reproduced or transmitted in any form or by any
electronic or mechanical means, including
photocopying, recording or by any information and
retrieval system, without the written permission of
the publisher and author, except where permitted by
law.
This novel is a work of fiction. Names,
characters, places and incidents are the product of
the author's imagination, or are used fictitiously.
Any resemblance to actual events, locales or persons,
living or dead, is purely coincidental.
ISBN: 978-1-925225-37-2
All rights reserved.

The device has not detonated.

Five simple words changed humanity's destiny, words which still hung in the air around the old man. The words had haunted the old man for years, mocking him, taunting him and assailing his conscience. It affected his sleep, his dreams. As his eyes failed him and the physical ailments became too much to bear, the words became that much more of a burden. The worst part of it all was that it was his fault, and only he knew it. The guilt of such knowledge could destroy any man.

His body rested in a hovering chair before a sea of monitors that covered the walls of the room around him. Originally designed as a temporary mobile medical support unit, the chair had become as much a part of him as the withered, drooping skin that covered his bones. Blue veins showed through his nearly transparent flesh, their spider web-like appearance giving the illusion of a shattered piece of glass. His eyes were sunken deep into his skull and ringed with the telltale signs of sleeplessness, but they still gleamed with the sharpness of intellect and cunning. Rows of tubes extended from the chair's arms and into his. They, more than his feeble old heart, pumped his blood and kept death at bay. Despite the indignities, he bore through it. He was a survivor, after all – he had lived through the end of the world three times now.

His mind drifted back to the days when he was a younger man, back when saving the world actually meant something. The first time that the world ended was when the oceans rose to reclaim the land and brought the massive Mother Kaiju with it. Mankind, initially overwhelmed by the gigantic creatures from the dark water, had been forced to seek shelter in domed city fortresses upon the islands that remained after the great flood. There,they had made their stand, the power of technology against the teeth and claws of the Mother Kaiju. Mankind held its own for some time, with the massive Kaiju unable to break through the thick walls of the city-states. Mankind and Kaiju settled into a stalemate, and for a time, an uneasy peace reigned.

That all changed with the arrival of the smaller foot soldiers of the Kaiju, the nine-foot long Dog Kaiju. Nor-wic fell first, and one by one, the city-states fell until only one remained. Lemura, the last standing city-state, had been the location of what humanity believed would be the last great fight between mankind and the Kaiju. The great beasts and their armies of lesser Kaiju had been fought back off its shores, trying to crush the city under their claws. A surprise attack by humans on a small island out in the middle of the ocean, followed by a sudden scientific breakthrough, had led to the destruction of the Kaiju Overmind.

This victory had seemed to shake the Kaiju to their core. The human race was given a brief reprieve and chance to rebuild from the Kaiju War. However, the stay of execution was all too brief as the Kaiju returned in force.

The second end was that of Lemura and all that had been rebuilt under the guidance of himself and Governor Yeltsin. When the Kaiju returned, they came like never before. There was no prolonged war, merely a series of quick decisive battles that thoroughly shattered what remained of the human race and wiped away most of the traces of the world before. What had once been a planet filled with light, laughter and hope had turned into a silent planet of death and sorrow.

Like many others, he had fled in those dark days. The world, as it was, had thought him dead. Instead of dying, however, he had retreated to a highly classified, and at the time being, unmanned research station buried deep in the Himalayas. The station was fully automated and equipped with not only a state-of-the-art AI, but also several drones designed to make life easy for anyone manning the remote location. There, he sat and planned, plotting to take back the world for humanity once and for all.

Often, he had considered reaching out to contact Yeltsin, to let the man know he was still alive, but something had kept him from it. Perhaps it had been fear, or something deeper, darker. If Yeltsin had known he was alive, the Minister would have spared no expense in bringing him back to his secured location beneath Lemura. He had wanted no part of the reconstruction or the desperate battles that came after, so he stayed in his station.

Though he had avoided Minister Yeltsin, he *had* contacted some of his old colleagues who had survived and passed along to them the design of a bomb that would destroy all of the Kaiju – and the Earth with it. Unfortunately, when Lemura finally fell, the device had yet to be fully completed. Yeltsin and a handful of survivors, holed up in Lemura's primary "last resort" bunker, took over the project, fulfilling his wishes without even realizing it. There, they continued work on the schematics, he had sent until a crude version of his bomb was online and tapped into the core of planet. His theory precluded the potential for cracking the core itself and triggering a chain reaction which would interrupt the spin of the planet, killing everything on it. He had waited and waited for Yeltsin to use the bomb and end them all, but for whatever reason, the minister-turned-governor never had. So he had languished, alone, while the world continued to spin... and Kaiju rampaged in their ceaseless orgy of destruction and carnage.

The device has not detonated.

He shivered at the memory, a cold chill running up his back. The chair was comfortable and set at the proper temperature to keep him warm, but no amount of technology could hold back the growing cold which was creeping through his body. Wracked with confusion and guilt, he had lain in the mobile support chair, his body mostly immobile, and his mind wandering back, thinking of the billions who had died. His sanity began to slip as his former colleagues died off in their forgotten bunkers.

Suddenly, and rather unexpectedly, a massive ship appeared in the skies over the Earth. He had recognized the craft, the moment of its arrival, though he doubted what he saw initially as he questioned his sanity. The ship was the *Argo*, which had been tasked to leave Earth behind and search for mankind's new home many years before. He had doubted his own eyes for a long time, even as the evidence piled up before him. Finally, he had accepted it for the truth and a new plan began to form in his still-active mind.

It was an easy matter to hack into its systems unnoticed and monitor what transpired on board the giant colony ship. The great ship had been sent out into the stars to find a new home for those it carried, the last hope of the human race. The mission to Alpha Centauri had been a complete and utter failure. A creature which had existed in Earth legends had already claimed the system as its own, and nobody on board the *Argo* wanted to fight for a new home. So they fled, leaving behind the potential new home to return to the bosom of mankind's origin.

He had not known whether to weep or laugh as he listened to the ship's hails over the various comm channels as the massive ship came into range. Its crew was completely unprepared to find the Earth still in the Kaiju's clutches upon their return. They set about gathering fresh supplies to leave the Sol system once more while also attempting to locate any survivors on the Earth's surface to take with them. He kept his silence throughout and merely watched their activities from the safety of his hidden facility, unwilling to leave his home. The thought of leaving Earth and allowing the Kaiju a true and complete victory over mankind sickened him, and he certainly was not foolish enough to believe that the *Argo* stood a decent chance of finding an Earth-like world to call home before the limited amount of supplies it could carry ran out.

He watched as the ruined streets of Lemura again ran red with the blood of humans as soldiers from the *Argo* discovered Yeltsin in his secret bunker and tried to take him with them to the stars. He had been *sure* that the former governor would not leave Earth without detonating the bomb he'd unwittingly helped build, but something must have gone terribly wrong. The *true* end had never come, and Yeltsin and the soldiers rescuing him disappeared beneath the giant foot of an enraged Mother Kaiju.

His years of studying the Overmind and the Kaiju had taught him the beasts' real nature. He knew of the great mother Kaiju that slumbered beneath the Earth's mantle, waiting to be awakened to take flight. The time of that awakening corresponded with the arrival of the *Argo.* Maybe her time to awake had come naturally, or maybe something about the great colony ship's experimental engines had stirred her the rest of the way out of her slumber? It hadn't mattered, not really. She had awaken with a ferocity born of hate and rage, and had rent the entire Pacific Basin asunder as she roused from her cocoon.

She took flight, reshaping the seabed as she rose. The planetary orbit was destabilized, and the moon shifted subtly due to this. Monstrous waves rose unbidden and crashed over every last bit of land still standing, including his hidden retreat. It had been a harrowing few weeks as he had worked to keep the water from flooding his home. Earth's orbit around the Sun was erratic now, and no computer model was in agreement, of what path it would take.

Miraculously, the planet itself survived. The damage done was beyond any sort of mending, though. He had prayed Yeltsin had set some sort of remote timer in order to detonate the bomb, but there had been no flash of heat and pain, no cleansing of the world, as the fires of bomb were unleashed. There was nothing but the mother of all Kaiju's birth pains as she broke free, and in an act which would shock the old man to his very core, engaged the *Argo* in space.

The massive ship fought against her with all it could bring to bear, but it was far from enough. Left with no other obvious choice, the ship's captain must have risked an unplotted leap across the galaxy, for the *Argo's* spatial jump bubble had formed around her. The Mother of All continued to fight, to rend into the colony ship, as it began to phase out of the solar system. The chaotic energy of the uncontrolled jump sliced into the massive Kaiju, wounding her grievously as the last hope for humanity disappeared into the stars.

After the colony ship was gone, vanished to only God knew where, her gargantuan body had fallen back to the world of her hibernation. Her death throes, which had lasted for many years, shook the Earth and stirred the oceans. Her children howled in anguish as she died. However, after she had died, they lived on. They hunted the last remnants of humanity, the few survivors who had been pushed to the brink of civilization and thrust into an age when club and spear were needed.

Everyday, he would ask the AI, which cared for his now-failing body the same question.

"The bomb? What of the bomb?"

The device has not detonated was always the same reply. The cold in his belly continued to grow, gnawing at the edges of his soul, and his sanity.

*****

Curri was never sure whether it was night or day. Nobody could, not anymore. Once, she had been told, you could look up and see the stars in the heavens clearly. Those days had long passed. Light and dark blended into a constant gray that hung over the Earth, due to the thick fog. There did not seem to be a difference between day and night any longer. A world of vibrant colors, once upon a time, Curri's environment was, and in her eyes, always had been one of a listlessness and constant gray.

She moved with the grace of a dancer across the jagged, uneven rocks. She was at least two miles from the cave where she and the others of her clan called home. No one else ever came out this far, unless things were so dire they had no other choice. Curri, like her father before her, was bold to the point of recklessness, and regularly partook in such excursions. It was her only escape from the pressing burdens of her duties. She could not recall when her life was different, when the world was alive with life and sound, but the images from her father's bedtime stories of her youth painted a picture which was so very unlike the world in which she lived. She often wondered if it was all simply a lie to get her to sleep on nights when the night terrors came.

The most vivid memory of her young life had been the day when the sky had burned and the ground had rumbled. Her parents told her that something had came home to Earth, though she couldn't quite remember what that something was supposed to have been. Her father had been so full of hope and excitement, his smile infectious on her young psyche. He was sure the time of the Kaiju was over, though that had deeply confused the young Curri. Whatever had arrived in the stars over the Earth would see to it, he said. He had continued to insist that they were saved even as he died in the collapsing tunnels of a world Curri could never quite grasp.

Curri's mother hadn't been as easily convinced, which saved both of their lives. The woman had done everything within her power to keep Curri levelheaded and aware that nothing might come from the thing in sky. As always, her mother had been right. All the thing in the sky had brought with it was more death, terror, and ultimately, sadness. Her clan called it The Day of the Burning Sky, and for good reason. The skies burned with a strange fire as the Earth beneath their feet shook endlessly. There had been nearly three hundred people fighting to stay alive on the island with them when it all began. Afterwards, there were less than fifty.

Curri's mother had managed to get her out only to die three years later of an infection caused after she had cut her foot on a rock. She had ignored the cut, even though Curri had insisted that she treat it. Something, though, had taken the fight out of her mother, who seemed lackluster in her efforts at keeping the clan alive. Despite their best healer's treatment, the fever took her mother from the clan.

Her mother had been a strong woman and taken over leadership of their tribe when her father perished. Losing her mother was simply too much for some of the less militaristic members of the clan. The clan split apart to go their separate paths in smaller groups. Thankfully, her mother's legacy was powerful enough, and over two dozen of the surviving military members of the clan had stayed with Curri, looking to her for hope and leadership. According to her makeshift calendar, that had been well over a decade before, though she had no idea just how accurate it was. Nobody could know for certain, though the general consensus among them was that her count was close enough.

The harshness of her life was evident. Her hands were callused, skin bruised and pale from lack of sunshine. She was rail-thin from lack of a proper diet and the difficulties of finding food safely. A lingering cough tickled her lungs and throat, remnants of the nasty bug, which had nearly killed her seven months before. Even so, she possessed an iron will and was both agile and strong. One had to be if one were going to keep breathing, keep surviving.

Curri remembered well her father's tales of the great cities like Pacifica, Altantica, and Lemura, though she had never seen them herself. They were gone now, like so much else from the world of the past. Ruined piles of rubble were all that remained of them all, mostly reclaimed by the seas when the Day of the Burning Sky had occurred. Her father *had* seen them while they were in their prime, filled with thousands of survivors and people. He had been a soldier during the last days of Lemura and fought in one of the last great battles upon its shores. He had been the steady rock when the city had fallen, when the Dog Kaiju had come to finish off the last remnants of humanity. It had been he who had led them under the city and out of it through secret tunnels known only to the military and the ruling elite. The majority of those who had left the tribe after her mother's death considered him a traitor, and said that he should have stayed and fought to the bitter end. The former military who had stayed behind, who were now what was left of her clan, knew better and told her so. They stayed away from the breakaway clan these days, content with their own ability to survive. She did find herself wondering if there were others like her out there, survivors. She desperately wanted to meet someone new.

Something splashed in the waters below her, tearing her away from her thoughts and back into the real world. Her keen eyes honed in on the fish struggling to free itself from the tiny pool of water in which it had become trapped. She smiled as she raised her spear. Her stomach gurgled hungrily as well-honed muscles pulled the spear in her hand back. She aimed one final time before she hurled it with all her strength.

She knew that her aim was true even before the spear struck the fish. It broke the surface of the water, impaling the fish perfectly. Dark red blood spilled out of the large fish and tainted the small pool. She hurried over to where the impaled fish lay. She knew she had to hurry and that time was short. The smell of blood, more often than not, drew a pack of Dog Kaiju into the area. She needed to be long gone before the creatures arrived. Curri couldn't risk them following her up the rocks and to her home in the caves in the jagged cliffs high above.

Curri knelt and picked up the dead fish and identified the predator almost instantly. She was pleased that it was a barracuda, though she had not seen one in a long time. The previous week's storm must have pushed them further in towards the land, she decided. She ran the spear completely through the barracuda to avoid damaging the meat of the large fish, her nimble hands working quickly. She pulled her large satchel off from her shoulder and carefully placed the fish inside. After a quick check to ensure that, the teeth of the dead fish could not damage the satchel, she shouldered the bag and grabbed her spear. She checked the barbed head and was satisfied that she had not damaged the precious instrument.

The sound of something sharp scraping against rock drew her undivided attention. The spear twirled in her hands as she pivoted on the balls of her feet, the point of the hunting tool pointing towards the sound. She dropped into a crouch as a small, dark shape emerged from behind a large rock. Her eyes narrowed as she recognized the juvenile Dog Kaiju as it began sniffing the air. Eyes locked onto her, and she snarled softly as the juvenile Kaiju hissed at her.

She recognized the tensing of the Kaiju's muscles just before he leapt at her. She pirouetted out of the way, the hunting spear twirling in her hands as the juvenile landed clumsily upon the jagged, uneven rock where she had been standing seconds before. The tip of the spear lashed out four times in rapid succession, each thrust cutting deeply into the Dog Kaiju's vulnerable front tendons. Off balance and lacking the strength to keep the weight on its legs, the juvenile fell onto the rocks, its mouth clacking shut violently as it crashed.

Curri was already moving again, skipping from one boulder to the next, as she moved into position behind the Dog Kaiju. Her balance was perfect. Her senses were honed from years of hardscrabble and the specter of death looming over her people on a daily basis. Another twist and she was behind the Dog Kaiju, balanced carefully atop a large flat rock. She found the vulnerable spot at the base of the young Kaiju's skull, and with a surety born of practice, drove the point home.

Her strike was perfect. The hindbrain of the Kaiju was located just above the end of the beast's spinal column in an area unprotected by the primary skull, where there were no arteries. Her spear tip, made from the same material which had once been used to create the armor of the Dogkiller suits of a people she could not identify with, severed the hindbrain from the primary. Every muscle in the juvenile's body spasmed and locked into place as paralysis spread throughout the creature. She managed to yank the spear back just before it would pierce the pulmonary artery of the Kaiju. Therefore, little blood splashed onto the rocks as the juvenile fell under her spear.

She looked around for any sign of another Dog Kaiju. She knew that the juveniles often acted as lone scouts to seek out and find any food source, and then passed along the news through a complicated tri-chambered olfactory gland in their throat. Every once in a while, however, a few juveniles would gather together and form their own pack. These packs were a danger to a lone hunter such as herself, because they often moved quieter and swifter than a pack filled with older, heavier Kaiju.

Curri was fortunate, this time. No other Dog Kaiju could be seen or heard. She waited for the Kaiju's last, shuddering breath to pass before she turned and hurried back to the cave she and the last remnants of her clan called home. It would be unwise to linger in this place of death.

*****

Curri slung the fish over her shoulder after pulling it from her gathering pouch. She had already cut off the head and tossed it away, leaving it for the seagulls which they sometimes hunted. She supposed such a gesture futile, since nobody had actually gotten close enough to kill one of the birds in months. Still, she knew that they had to be nesting somewhere nearby. The island was big, but it wasn't that big. She nearly drooled at the thought of finding a clutch of seagull eggs.

Higgins met her as she strolled into the mouth of the cave. Once, he had been a giant of a man, nearly seven feet tall and pure muscle. Years of malnourishment had left him skinnier than he had ever been before. He was still bigger than everyone else in the clan was, however. He stood, towering over her, frowning at her with a look of disapproval. "I thought you were going to wait before you went out again."

He might have been attractive, if not for the scars covering his body, but she could never think of him in *that* way. In the years since her parents' deaths, he had watched over her, helping her grow into her role as leader of the clan. He was her rock, dependable and sturdy, even if he was a judgmental jerk and full of himself at times.

More than a few of his scars came keeping her alive and not, as one would presume, from the Kaiju Wars. A jagged gash ran across his left cheek, a reminder of the time where he stood in for her during a duel for power within the clan and his opponent got in a lucky swing of a knife before Higgins broke the man's spine. The charred flesh of his own back served as another memento of just how devoted to her he was. When fire fell from the sky during the dark times, as the blue above turned to gray, he had sheltered her with his own body until they could crawl the last few feet into the cave they were racing for when all Hell broke loose. His right hand was missing its little finger, his left ear was mauled from a clash with a Dog Kaiju, and long scars ran the lengths of his legs from yet another clash with the lesser Kaiju. To say that Higgins was tough would be a gross understatement. Curri, however, was not intimidated by him in the least, though some in the clan were deathly afraid of him.

"We have to eat, Higgins," she reminded him yet again. "Hunger can kill us just as well as the Dogs can, just that would be slower and more agonizing. Take a look outside, why don't you? There's one hell of a storm rolling in. Should be here in an hour or two at the most. It'll wipe away any scent I might have left before the Dogs have a chance to try to track me here. If they even find the body."

With a grunt, Higgins reached for the fish she held out to him. Curri jerked the fish away from him suddenly, holding it beyond his reach. She scowled at him. "If you're going to complain about me getting food for us all, you get to eat last."

"The Dog Kaiju comes closer to finding our little haven here every time you venture out. There is more at stake here than just your piddling little pride," he told her as he retreated a step.

"My pride?" Curri snapped. "You think I'd risk all our lives just to show how great a leader I am?"

"Yes, your pride. And you do seem to want to prove yourself to the others, but you have no need of doing so. Everyone is well aware of your prowess with a spear, and nobody questions your bravery. The tribe would have starved long ago without you."

Curri huffed at Higgins, giving him a wide berth as she walked past him into the cave. Deep within, the others waited for her.

Higgins followed her to the doorway. It was an old door, built during the opening days of the Kaiju Wars. It was heavy and was, once upon a time, protected by a massive locking mechanism, though its servomotors no longer functioned. The tribe relied upon brute strength to open and close it these days, since the combination of salty air and a constant moisture had turned it to near-solid rust. Higgins alone could perform the task on his own. Otherwise, it took three grown men to lock the door in place. Curri waited as he took hold of the door and heaved, moving it mere inches to one side. It took Higgins several more such displays of his strength to open it enough for them to enter. He then stayed behind to close it once more as she continued on.

There were more than a few entrances and exits within the network of caves in the mountain, but this one was the one closest to the ocean, and therefore, it was kept sealed at all times. Had Higgins not been waiting on her upon her arrival, Curri would have needed to wait until whoever was on watch further down the tunnel heard the echoes of her metal-tipped spear clanging on it. Folks felt better with the door closed, though if the Dog Kaiju found their home, its presence would likely only buy them an hour at most. Thankfully, the cave didn't solely depend upon the armored door to keep it safe. The cave was remote and hidden, and the laziness and lack of single-mindedness of the Kaiju upon the death of their mother added greatly to their safety.

The tribe called this place "The Cave," but in truth, it was a bunker left over from the world before. Or rather, part of a breached one. Oil lamps lined the walls of its passages instead of powered lights, filling the air with a sooty smell that reminded them all everyday of the horrid world they now lived in. There was very little which remained of the former bunker which they had not scavenged for parts or tried to repair. The people of the tribe had not lost so much as to forget such things, but neither did they have the parts, or some cases the skills, to make them all functional again.

One of the relative few people who had the skills to fix just about everything greeted her as she emerged from the shadows of the corridor. Matan, a small, diminutive man who looked as if his last meal had occurred sometime in the previous decade, greeted her with a smile from behind the table. His warm welcome eased the tension between Curri's shoulders some. His intelligent eyes drifted from her face to the fish which she had clutched in her hand. His smile grew slightly bigger.

"Welcome back," Matan said, as he inclined his head in her direction. He pushed aside the technical drawings which were spread out upon the table. "I guess we'll all be having a bit more for dinner tonight than kelp and moss."

Higgins had caught up to her and stood behind Curri as she stopped to speak with Matan.

"Any luck?" she asked.

Matan's laugh was a bitter one. "I'm an engineer, not a miracle worker. I can only do so much, you know."

Curri frowned. Matan had been at work on the cave's comm system for months. When they had first relocated here, he told her he could probably get it up and running, even if most of the other systems in the cave were beyond hope. She had entrusted him with the task of getting it working again and let him stay inside, where it was safe from any danger. He had not foraged for goods since then, and was still eating his share. So far, he had failed, and her patience – and the patience of the others – was beginning to grow thin.

"We need that comm system up and running," Higgins growled from behind her.

Matan sat his book down in front of him, spreading his hands in a gesture of peace. "I'm doing the best I can with what I have at hand," he said, his voice earnest. "The power cell Curri brought in from that torn apart Dog Killer suit a while back helped a lot, but look... I am pretty much rebuilding things from scratch here, and making up things on the fly to get the system operational, or as close to operational as I can make it. I'm close, I can feel it. I swear. Just give me a little more time."

"You have time," Higgins reminded the sharp-nosed younger man with a pointed look at the book he had been reading. "You have plenty of time, apparently."

Adjusting his battered and taped glasses, Matan shrugged. He refused to let the giant towering behind Curri press him further. "I've got one last thing I can try this evening. Kind of a last-ditch thing, I suppose. If it works, it works. If not... well, there's nothing else I can do until I get more parts. And the problem is..."

"You don't know what type of parts you need until you try it," Higgins finished for him. He grunted but let the issue rest.

"Just do what you can," Curri instructed him, trying to keep the weariness from her tone. "Higgins and I have a fish to clean. We'll catch you later."

Matan nodded at them as they walked on past him, deeper into the cave.

The corridor opened in a wide room with a high ceiling. Inside was the makeshift camp of the tribe. Numerous tents filled the space between its walls. They were built for privacy more than for anything else, so that the members of the tribe had some space they could retreat to when they needed it, rather than venturing alone into the other parts of the cave.

A small crowd gathered around Curri and Higgins as they set about preparing the fish to be cooked. Rebecca and her two children were there. Nanci was redheaded like her mother while Buck's hair was a much darker brown. John was there too. The silver cross he always wore dangled from a rusting chain about his neck as he stood next to Dave and Luthor. Everyone was excited about having some meat with their evening meal, regardless of how small a portion it was going to be when divvied out equally.

The smell of the fish being cooked made Curri's mouth water but she didn't plan on taking a share of it herself. There were others in the tribe, and not just the children, who needed it more. Leigh was pushing seventy and her health was far from good. Curri had seen the kind of sickness the older woman had before and knew Leigh would likely perish in the coming weeks or months, but she refused to give up hope on the older woman.

After the tribe's meal, Curri left Higgins to attend to the day-to-day matters of the tribe and assigning the duties for the next day. Every member of the clan worked, whether it was working at repairing the tattered clothing, they all wore, cleaning and caring for the latrines, taking guard shifts at the key entrances, or more specialized projects like the comm system Matan was working on.

Curri ducked down one of the corridors leading out of the cave's central area and headed for Matan's workshop. He was already there working, when she arrived. A plate of untouched kelp with a lump of fish sat on the table next to him.

"Matan?" she said, startling him.

He jumped and spun around to face her, an old world revolver leveled at her chest. His cheeks flushed red as he recognized her and the fear in on face shifted to embarrassment.

"Does that thing even work?" she taunted him.

"It does now," he answered, tucking the pistol into a holster on his belt. "I finally cracked the lock to the cave's armory yesterday."

"W-what?" Curri stammered in disbelief.

"Oh yeah," Matan chuckled. "I suppose, I forgot to mention that earlier. Your giant friend was sort of imposing. Must have slipped my mind."

"Matan, are you telling me that we have weapons again? Real weapons?"

He nodded excitedly. "That we do. There are even a couple of Dog Killer suits in there. Not sure if they are functional or not yet, as I haven't had time to test them, but they look to be in decent shape. I just figured the comm system took priority so I have been mainly continuing to focus on it."

Curri gritted her teeth and forced herself not to be angry. She knew how task oriented Matan could be when given a project. "Okay," she said. "We'll do an inventory of the armory tomorrow and start handing out weapons to those we know that can be trusted to use them correctly. I'm sure Higgins will want to handle that anyway," she paused, moving to stand next to where he sat. "So did the test you were going to try with the comm work?"

"Hold on," Matan said as he flipped through the frequency settings again. He paused and changed the position of the wire. "That's weird... it shouldn't be doing that."

"Doing what, Matan?" Curri asked.

"I put it to 'receive only' for settings, but for some reason, I'm broadcasting instead," Matan tried to explain. "How to put this... ah! It's like when you're out hunting and you want to watch and wait, but instead of watching, you're just yelling out into the dark and stomping along the rocks, making as much noise as you can."

"But still, you got it working," Curri said with a grin.

"The problem is that I'm not really sure who's listening."

*****

There was a hissing noise as a the tube implanted into the doctor's sternum finished injecting his heart with his daily dose of cardiac medication. With a soft *pop,* it disengaged itself and was retracted back inside the hover chair. His broken body lay undisturbed for a moment as the medicine began to take hold. His skin wasn't quite as pale as it had been a few moments earlier and he felt somewhat better. He knew the feeling wouldn't last. It never did. All the technology and drugs at his disposal were nothing more than a means of prolonging his life, not cure the old age that he battled every day. The medication barely kept the cancer which ate away at him at bay. His time was running out. The drugs were losing their effectiveness. His natural antibodies in his blood were beginning to build up a resistance to them.

One of the research station's half-dozen maintenance drones stood nearby. A pincer-like metal hand clutched a glass of water. Tiny flecks of various minerals floated in the liquid. They, too, were just another part of the doctor's massive daily routine of keeping death away. He wasn't sure yet if it was a placebo effect or that they actually helped, but the vitamin-infused water seemed to help a bit, so he was reluctant to give up on that treatment.

"I'm ready," he thought through the neural interface in his brain and the drone moved towards him. It tipped the glass up to his mouth and allowed him to drink from it, pulling it away when he gave the signal that he was done.

"Thank you, Clint," the doctor conveyed to the drone. It was not aware, unlike the station's AI, but when you were as alone as he was, the doctor believed it paid to keep up such things. They were necessary, for his own sake, to keep him from not going mad from his isolation. He had named each of the station's drones long ago and thought of them as companions more than he thought of them as machines. "That will be all."

Clint turned and left the room, the drone's heavy footfalls clanging on the metal floor as it went.

The doctor closed his eyes and he prepared himself for sleep. The work cycle of the day was over and all that needed to be done to buy him one more day, Lord willing, had been completed.

The cold, hollow voice of the station's AI called to him. "Doctor?"

"What is it, Gregory?" he responded, exhausted from his treatments and ready for the day to be over.

"You wished to be notified at once if I detected transmissions from others like yourself. I believe I have done so."

The doctor's eyes snapped open. "Where?"

"On the remainder of the island state of Alantica. It is coming from its eastern most shoreline."

"Patch the signal through at once," he ordered and listened in utter shock, as for the first time in years, he heard another human voice calling out to him.

"This is Matan. Is there anyone out there that can hear me? I repeat, is there anyone out there?"

The doctor's lips cracked, droplets of blood forming upon them, as they twisted into the closest semblance of a smile he could muster. "At last," he muttered. "Gregory, get the drones ready. It could be that our wait is finally over."

****

Curri nearly fell over on top of Matan where he sat at his work desk with the jerry-rigged pieces of the comm system in front of him as a raspy voice answered his calls.

"Mr. Matan, this is Research Station... Hope. I copy you loud and clear. Over."

Matan glanced up at Curri. "What do I do?"

"Answer him," she urged Matan. "Hurry! Before something goes wrong and we lose the signal!"

"This is Matan of the Lannier tribe, Hope. Are we ever happy to hear from you."

A dry, sickly laugh answered Matan's word. "I think it can be safely said that the feeling is mutual, Mr. Matan. It's been some time since someone has activated the global comm net."

Curri leaned over Matan, "What's your name?" she asked almost breathlessly. "To whom are we speaking?"

A long period of silence followed her question.

"Did we lose the signal?" she asked Matan, growing anxious.

"Nope. We still have it, I think."

"You'll have to forgive me," the voice replied in a near-breathless tone. "Old age. You may address me as Dr. Bach."

Curri and Matan exchanged a quick, equally shocked glance.

"Dr. Bach?" Matan asked. "As in *the* Dr. Bach?"

"One and the same. Rumors of my death have been greatly exaggerated, suffice to say."

"It's an honor to speak with you, sir," Matan smile. "Where is your facility located? Are there many with you, sir? Can you reach our location for extraction?"

"Hold on. Slow down, young man. I am sure we'll cover everything in due course," the doctor told them. "And please keep it to only one question at a time please. As to where I am located, I'll merely say, it is very far away. I am alone here, other than several worker drones originally designed to maintain this facility. And sadly, no. I have no means of dispatching *that* sort of help to you."

Curri watched Matan's shoulders slump.

"Are there many of you in your tribe, Matan?" the doctor asked.

"Hold on for one second, Doctor," Matan said as Curri gestured for him to mute the broadcast. It took Matan a moment to realize that Curri wanted to be able to speak without the doctor hearing them. When Matan confirmed that he had muted the broadcast, she spoke.

"How do we knew he's for real? I mean, what if he's just part of another tribe and they're looking to take what we have?"

"What do we have, Curri?" Matan argued, "Some kelp, rusting walls around us, and packs of Dog Kaiju that gets closer to finding us every day?"

"We have *us,*" she said. "If he's lying, and there are soldiers at that station with him, they might want slaves, or worse, breeding stock. No matter how tempting it is to work with him, we can't endanger the group recklessly by just handing out details on our strength and location."

"If the system he's using is anywhere near as good as what I think it is, Curri, he already knows exactly where we are."

Curri muttered a string of curses. "The real Dr. Bach was supposed to have died before the great beast fell back to the Earth from the stars during the time of the burning skies," she pointed out.

"I believe him, Curri," Matan stared at her. "It would take someone pretty important to still have equipment like what he's using to talk with us. I mean, look at this. Even with this piece of junk I'm using, I can tell he's got access to the whole global net. He caused our comm unit to seek out him, and not the other way around. That takes some serious power and knowledge."

"I still don't like this," Curri admitted, "but I guess you're right. What choice do we have but to trust him if we want to find out anything about what's really left out there?"

Matan reopened the channel without waiting on her to say more. "There are around two dozen of us, sir. Mostly civilians, but a few soldiers from the war."

"And are you armed?" the ancient sounding voice asked them. "My readings show that you are located in the old Alantica tunnel system. To be more specific, the coastal defense bunker there."

Giving Curri an *I told you so* look, Matan answered. "We are armed. Mostly small arms, but we've recently discovered a few Dog Killer suits at the location and we are beginning work to see if we can get them online. Are you suggesting that we make our way to your location, sir?"

"Negative, Lannier tribe. However, I believe I know a means by which you can help us both."

****

The entirety of the Lannier tribe gathered around Curri, Higgins, and Matan. Curri had called the meeting to discuss what to do in the face of the knowledge that they were no longer alone. That knowledge was met with an equal degree of excitement and fear by most as she told them of what Dr. Bach asked of them.

"Dr. Bach is aware of our situation here. He is alone and unable to act himself from his location, but he believes that the island of Lemura holds something that will help us all against the Kaiju. He has asked us to make our way there under his guidance. There is a bunker on Lemura much like this one, only much stronger and according to his data, still fully operational. If what he says is true, we would finally be safe from the Kaiju."

"Ain't no place left that's safe!" someone in the crowd shouted.

"The bunker there is *intact,*" Curri repeated herself, "And likely fully stocked. We'd have food, power, and more weapons. Compared to this place, it would be like a fortress."

"I agree," Higgins cut in. "If this Dr. Bach is on the level, it would mean a whole new life for us all. We'd have access to sensors and be able to see the Kaiju's movements around the bunker. There would be no more living in fear like we do now. More than that, this place he wants to head for would be stocked up with medications as well. Those are something we all need. How many have we lost to simple infections? The medical facilities of a bunker like the one he's talking about would be worth the risks of the journey alone."

Zack stepped forward from the crowd. He was a wiry man in his later twenties, lean and hard. Zack was one of the Lannier tribe's few full-out warriors, and he worked for Higgins. "You're talking like this journey is no big deal. Have you forgotten just how far away Lemura is, or how many Kaiju, both Dog and Mother, will be between us and there?"

"Matan here has managed to unlock *this* bunker's armory. We are no longer lacking for firepower," Higgins answered Zack's challenge. "I wouldn't have agreed to let Curri suggest any of this if I didn't think we had a chance at some of us making it to Lemura alive."

"And those are the key words, aren't they?" Zack argued. "*Some* of us, making it there alive."

Matan put a hand on Higgins' chest, stopping the big man from plowing forward at Zack. "The risk is worth the gain," he said to Zack calmly. "Unless we want to die here, living as we are, this is our only chance of finding something better. Not just for us adults, but for the tribe's children too. Think of them, Zack."

Curri could see that Matan had won over Rebecca and the other parents of the tribe with that simple statement.

"Fine," Zack glanced around at the crowd. "Let's put it to a vote and be done with it."

"Curri is our leader," Higgins snarled. "What she says goes."

"No!" Curri shook her head. "This is something we all must decide together. A vote is the best way to settle things. All in favor say *aye.*"

The chorus of voices in agreement was so loud, they echoed in the cave. Only Zack and a couple of the others gathered kept quiet.

"It's decided then," Curri smiled. "Higgins, Matan. Get started with the preparations. I want everyone ready to move out, come dawn."

****

The cave was a beautiful mess of chaos as folks darted about gathering up their meager belongings or helping those who were sick, like Leigh, getting ready for the coming journey. Higgins, Zack, and the tribe's other warriors were off with Matan, in the cave's armory, preparing as well. She supposed that was where she needed to be as well, but the sight of her people so active and filled with hope kept her rooted to the spot where she stood watching them.

"Curri?" Nanci called, climbing up the jagged rocks to the overhang where she stood. "Do you really think we'll make it?"

She reached down and helped the small, red-haired girl up onto the rocks beside her.

"I hope so," Curri brushed a rogue strand of that red hair from the girl's face as she spoke.

"It feels like we're finally going home," Nanci smiled.

"I suppose we are," Curri laughed. "You know what I can't wait for?"

"What?" Nanci giggled with excitement.

"A shower," Curri laughed too. "I can almost remember what those feel like. It'll be so strange to be clean again."

"Curri!" Matan shouted from beneath them. He motioned for her to come down and join him.

"Sorry, Nanci. I have to go," Curri ruffled the hair atop Nanci's head. "Duty calls."

Curri met Matan at the entrance to the corridor leading to the cave's armory where he waited on her. She could tell from his expression that the news was going to be good and thought this was something she could certainly get in the habit of happening.

"The Dog Killers *are* functional," Matan informed her. "Higgins has experience using the suits, so we're good there too. He should be able to give a crash course to whoever we stick in the other four."

"Four? I thought you said there was only a couple."

"Yeah, we lucked out again," Matan beamed. "In the meantime, as we decide who the pilots are going to be, Higgins is busy handing out weapons to the folks he trusts with them. It looks like this place has enough ammo in it for us to fight a small war with."

"Good," Curri said. "Odds are we are going to need it out there."

"But it gets even better than that," Matan looked ready to burst. "With Dr. Bach's help over the comm, I was able to access some areas of the cave we could never get into before. Guess what the good doctor led us to?"

"No idea and you'd better not try to make me guess," Curri warned him.

"Two APCs!" Matan cackled like a madman.

"What's an APC?" Curri asked.

She could see she had completely taken the thunder out of his surprise as Matan sighed.

"APC stands for Armored Personnel Carrier. They're like big armored trucks, Curri. It means we won't have to walk. The sick won't be slowing us down."

"Oh, that's great," Curri feigned excitement, still not fully getting it.

Still disappointed, Matan led her down the corridor towards the armory. "Just follow me. I'll show them to you."

****

As the weak light of the rising sun seeped through the clouds over Alantica, the Lannier tribe left the cave behind. Curri sat in the driver's compartment of the lead APC. She watched as Matan worked the vehicle's controls. Curri had no idea who Matan had entrusted to driving the other one, as both Higgins and Zack, along with the other more combat experienced men, were suited up in Dog Killer suits that ran alongside the APCs. She was beginning to question her decision of having the tribe move out so fast. More time for everyone to learn how to use the new weapons and vehicles they had been blessed with might have been a good thing. But according to Dr. Bach, the sooner they were "on the road," the better.

The APCs had their own comm gear as did the Dog Killer suits so Matan no longer required the bulky, jerry-rigged comm unit he had built from bits and pieces scattered about the ruins of the cave anymore. The doctor had provided them with a downloaded map detailing the path of least resistance between them and their current destination, which was the heart of Atlantica. There, they were to ditch the APCs as something called a Trident would be waiting on them. According to Higgins and Matan, a Trident was another type of old world vehicle that flew through the air. They would need it to reach their final goal in Lemura.

Curri stared out the APC's windshield at the wasteland Matan drove them through. The distance to Altantica proper was not far from the cave. With the APCs pushed to their max, their ETA to the waiting Trident was less than two hours.

Each APC was equipped with a topside, turret mounted weapon. Higgins had assigned Daniel to man theirs. Every few minutes, a lone Dog Kaiju or a small pack of the creatures would come into view. They loped across the sands on thick, muscled legs, their yellow eyes blazing with rage and fury, lips parted in hungry snarls. For the most part, the Dog Kaiju simply could not keep up with the APCs and they were left quickly behind. When the attack came, no one was expecting it.

The APCs were barreling down a strip of real roadway towards Atlantica. The road was lined by hills of sand that stirred and blew in the wind as they passed by. The Dog Kaiju they had encountered earlier must have somehow been able to communicate with those ahead of the APCs because the monsters laid a trap for them. Ahead of the lead APC, dozens of the Dog Kaiju came pouring onto the road. Cursing, Matan slammed on the vehicle's brakes. There were too many of the things to plow through. Their numbers and strength would stop the APC dead in its tracks if they tried. The second APC braked behind them and Curri heard Daniel open up on the creatures with the 105 caliber guns on its turret. The heavy rounds tore into the ranks of the creatures. Curri watched as one of the Dog Kaiju's head exploded from a lucky shot, spraying fragments of bone and chunks of brain matter onto the road. Another pair of the things was caught at waist level by Daniel's stream of fire. Their bodies jerked and danced as their stomachs and chests were punctured by too many bullets to count. They were disemboweled where they stood, their legs blown out from under them, before their corpses flopped to lay still on the road. Still, the beasts came. They surged forward towards the APC, as an unstoppable mass of razor teeth and claws. Curri screamed at the sight of them. More Dog Kaiju appeared at the tops of the hills lining the road and began sprinting down the shifting sand towards the two APCs, as yet another mass filled the roadway behind them. The Dog Killer troops, led by Higgins, moved to engage them.

"We have to get out of here!" Curri yelled at Matan as a Dog Killer lumbered in front of the window of their APC. Curri didn't know if it was Higgins in the suit or not, but whoever it was, he clearly knew how to operate the armor. Twin rocket launchers rose from the Dog Killer's shoulders and spat destruction at the Dog Kaiju. The explosion from the volleys ripping into the Kaiju's forward ranks shook the APC. Curri covered her eyes against the intense light of the blast.

Higgins' voice came over the APC's comm. "All units, concentrate fire on the Dog Kaiju mass in front of the vehicles. We have to break through or it's all over, right here, right now."

Curri blinked her stinging eyes, trying to clear her vision. The other Dog Killers came running up beside the APC she sat in, passing it on both sides. They threw themselves into the Kaiju, charging forward to meet them. Their mag-cannons chattered and boomed, drenching the road in Kaiju blood.

One of the Dog Killers stumbled as a Kaiju leaped onto its back. Sparks flew as the thing's long claws raked the suit's shoulders. Two more Kaiju tackled the Dog Killer, taking it to the ground. The screams of the man inside the suit could be heard over the shared channel of the APCs and the power-armored troops.

"Somebody kill that channel!" Higgins' voice ordered.

Matan shook himself as if waking up from a nightmare. His fingers flew over the controls in front of him and the sound of the man screaming vanished just as it reached a crescendo. Curri saw one of the Kaiju attacking the downed suit thrust a hand clutching what looked to be part of the man's spine high into the air over its head in victory.

"There are too many of them!" Mark shouted over the comm. link. He must have been driving the second APC, because even as he cried out, it shifted into reverse. Its massive wheels peeled out on the roadway as it shot backwards into the growing mass of Kaiju behind it. The APC made it a good distance into the things before their numbers bogged it down. The Kaiju swarmed over it like ants, climbing up onto its sides and top. Matan was using the external sensors of their own APC to view the carnage and Curri watched with him. The second APC's gunner was yanked from his turret or rather his upper half was. Long, bloody strands of intestines stretched from where one of the Kaiju held the man's twitching torso back into the inside of the APC where his lower half still remained. Several of the Dog Kaiju were working together to tear into the top of the second APC, peeling back its armor as if they were opening up a tin can.

The gun turret above, and behind Matan and Curri on their own APC, fell silent. There were screams from the rear compartment as Curri turned to glance through the open interior doorway and saw blood running down the steps of the short ladder leading up to the turret.

An explosion lit the road ahead of them again. One of the Dog Killers had self-destructed among the Kaiju there.

"That's it!" Higgins yelled over the comm. "Get your asses moving, people. That opening ain't gonna stay there forever!"

The sacrifice made by the Dog Killer had cleared a path through the Kaiju. Matan stomped on the accelerator and their APC shot forward like an armored missile. It bounced over the smoldering corpses of the Kaiju littering the road and then was clear of the combat zone. A loud clang sounded from its rear followed by a second. The APC lurched as if a great weight had been added to it. Its engine whined in protest, straining, but the vehicle kept moving, if a little slower.

"What the devil?" Matan shrieked, not taking his eyes off the road ahead.

"It's us!" Higgins' voice boomed over the comm. "Zack and I are catching a ride with you!"

"Roger that!" Matan said. "Shifting all power to compensate!"

Curri noticed that Matan still had the sensors trained to the APC's rear. There was no sign of the second APC as they sped onward.

"We. . ." Higgins said, and then paused, swallowing, "...we lost the others."

****

Curri felt relief wash over her as the city of Atlantica came into view. Higgins and Zack were back to running alongside the APC. The vehicle, as powerful as it was, simply could not bear the prolonged strain of carrying the Dog Killers without its engine burning out.

There had been several more Dog Kaiju attacks, but none as devastating as the first. Matan piloted the APC through the ruins of Atlantica proper, guiding it around the various overturned and mauled tanks, APCs, and civilian transports that filled its streets. Thankfully, for the moment, there was no sign of any more Dog Kaiju.

Matan didn't stop the APC as they reached the fence enclosing the hangar area that Dr. Bach's directions had guided them to. Instead, he drove into the fence and through it before finally coming to a stop.

There, before them, sat a Trident. The ship was several times the size of APC they rode in and its armored hull bristled with weapon enhancements. Its hull gleamed in the dim rays of the cloud-obscured sunlight.

"Wow," Curri breathed, "so that's what a Trident is."

Matan flashed her a grin as she unfastened the straps of her seat and moved into the APC's rear section. Curri worked her way through the survivors of tribe Lannier, checking on them and assuring them that the worst was over. Rebecca sat with Nanci, and Buck held close to her in a tight embrace. Curri put on a smile for them as she helped them out of the APC. Higgins and Zack stood watch over the small group as they disembarked from the APC and boarded the Trident. By the time, Curri got onboard herself, Matan was already in the pilot seat, conversing with Dr. Bach over the ship's comm. From what she could overhear, Matan was arguing with Bach and telling the doctor that none of them had the skills required to fly the Trident.

Curri plopped into the co-pilot's seat next to Matan as Dr. Bach's voice said, "Don't panic. I planned for this, Matan. I can fly the ship from here. All you have to do is be on it when it lifts off."

Matan touched the comm controls. "Higgins, is everyone loaded up?"

"Everyone except Zack and me. We have Kaiju inbound. There are two packs of the things closing in from the east and north. We're laying down suppressive fire now."

"Belay that," Matan told them with a smirk. "Just get in here. Now!"

"You heard the man!" Higgins shouted before the comm. went silent. A brief moment later, Zack's voice called out, "We're in!

Get us the hell out of here already! Those Kaiju are hauling butt and closing in fast!"

Without any prompting from Matan, the Trident came to life around them. Her engines roared and she raised herself from the landing area in a sharp, vertical take off.

Matan let out a whoop as the Trident slashed its way into the gray clouds, leaving Atlantica behind it.

****

The Trident's flight was a short one. Dr. Bach guided it remotely to the exact location of the bunker the Lannier tribe had set out to find. The bunker was easy to spot from the air, long before the Trident touched down outside of its entrance. It lay half-exposed in the middle of a main street, chunks of the pavement covering it torn away and the scars of gigantic claw marks marring the metal of its uncovered roof. Dog Kaiju were everywhere. Missiles streaked from the Trident as it descended, clearing the area around the bunker with explosions of fire and shrapnel.

Matan popped the rear cargo bay doors of the Trident remotely from the cockpit as Curri stood next them. "Everyone out!" she ordered. "Run for those doors!"

The two Dog Killers containing Higgins and Zack were first through the door. They took up secure positions and laid a withering hailstorm of gunfire into the new swarms of Kaiju emerging from the surrounding alleys and buildings with everything they had. Large caliber rounds blew snarling Dog Kaijus to shreds as they bounded towards the Trident and bunker.

Curri and Rebecca were the last two off the Trident. Rebecca carried Nanci in her arms, sweating from the effort, as she sprinted for the bunker doors that slid open before the other members of the

Lannier tribe, who were already reaching them. Curri followed after her with Buck in tow. She dragged the boy along by his right hand, forcing him to keep pace with her.

Higgins and Zack had begun to make their own retreat, edging towards the bunker as they kept firing. Curri could see that the two of them weren't going to make it at the rate they were moving. She'd learned to tell the two suits apart during the trip to Atlantica. Zack was closest to the bunker, but even he was too far away to have any hope of making it there in time. She watched as Higgins and Zack slowed and adjusted themselves to stand back to back. Their Mag-cannons blazed, killing Dog Kaiju by the dozens, but for every one of the beasts that fell, three more seemed to take its place. Lemura was teeming with the things and there seemed to be no end to the creatures' numbers.

She watched as the Dog Kaiju blocked her view of her protector. She could hear the hard hammering of the mag-cannon over the snarls of the Dogs, though, and she held out hope for the two Dogkiller suits to make it to the safety of the bunker. Her heart beat wildly in her chest as she ran, while trying to make it to the bunker doors.

The harsh sounds of the mag-cannon abruptly died behind her.

There was nothing Curri could do to help them, however. Tears formed in her eyes as she continued to run, her legs pumping beneath her and her breath coming in ragged gasps. The bunker doors thudded shut after she and Buck passed through them. Curri dropped to her knees, fighting to catch her breath as sobs racked her trembling body.

A disembodied voice echoed inside the bunker. It was Matan's. "I'm sorry, Curri. Higgins and Zack are gone."

"Where are you?" Curri gasped, getting to her feet and standing as the other survivors of the Lannier tribe huddled just inside the bunker's entrance around her. The loss of Zack was bad enough, but losing Higgins nearly broke her spirit completely. Though she had butted heads with the man since she had assumed the mantle of leadership, she had relied upon him to be her guide, her rock. She looked at the survivors of her tribe. She had to be their rock, as she always had before.

"I'm on the Trident," Matan told her. "I've taken over control of the bunker's internal comm with the help of Dr. Bach. He. . . he said that he was giving me the chance to say good bye."

"Matan!" Curri wailed at the bunker's ceiling. "We're safe! What are you doing?"

She could almost see him shaking his head at the Trident's controls.

"No, Curri, you're not. Nobody is safe. Dr. Bach lied to us. As strong as that bunker may be, the Mother Kaiju are coming. All of them. Every one that's still alive, that is. They'll tear the bunker apart."

"What? Why?" Curri rasped, tears streaming along the curves of her cheeks to splatter on the metal floor at her feet.

"Dr. Bach never intended for us to find somewhere safe. He was using us, Curri. Inside that bunker is a weapon, some sort of bomb from what I gather, that can cleanse the Earth of the Kaiju, Mother and Dog alike. He wants you to detonate it for him."

"Oh, but you will," Dr. Bach's voice purred over the intercom. "You'll see."

"Matan!" Curri cried out. "Matan, where are you?"

"He's rather busy right now, I'm afraid," Dr. Bach said. "You see, the Kaiji *know* we are about to end them and their kind forever. Your friend will die in a blaze of glory along with the war drones I have dispatched to aid him, but rest assured, his sacrifice will help to buy you the time you require. Now, calm yourself and listen. Here is what I need you to do. . ."

"I won't help you," Curri's tone was icy, her determination etched in stone.

"Curri," Dr. Bach said in a much gentler manner. "This is the end. You have only two choices now. Let your people die in vain, as the Kaiju rip their way inside the bunker and tear all of you limb from limb before their teeth strip the flesh from your bones, or to do as I say. I do not offer you hope of escape. There is none to be had. What I offer is a quick, noble death to the remainder of your tribe, but with your sacrifice, you will bring vengeance upon the Kaiju for all mankind. The bomb I have designed lies within the center of the bunker in which you reside. You merely need to reach it and activate its countdown. The device itself will finish things from there."

"And Matan? " Curri asked. "Is it not in your power to spare him?"

"You do not comprehend the magnitude of the device I am asking you to activate. It will eradicate the Earth and all of the Kaiju with it. Even if I wished to spare your friend, I cannot. The class of Tridents he's piloting was not built for space travel."

Curri glanced about her. Rebecca and Nanci were weeping openly. All the others of the Lannier tribe, too, were frozen by fear and despair.

"Choose now, Curri," Bach urged her. "Revenge or a painful, meaningless death at the claws of the creatures outside these doors?"

"Curri?" Rebecca asked.

"Kill them," Buck spoke up through his own tears. "Kill every last one of those monsters."

Curri met the boy's eyes and nodded.

"Which way?" She snapped at Dr. Bach over the comm.

"Good," he laughed. "I knew you would be up to the challenge at hand."

****

Matan was quickly able to discern how the Trident functioned, and after a brief moment of sheer panic when he nearly flew the aircraft into the ground, he managed to turn the autopilot off. He carefully swung the craft around and climbed high into the sky. He peered down at the waters below and grimaced as he spotted the numerous Mother Kaiju stalking the ruined city. The people in the bunker didn't stand a chance, he realized. Curri and the others would die.

One lone Trident stood little chance against a Mother. An entire wing of Tridents might be able to stop one or two Mothers. Against this many, Matan wasn't sure he would even be able to hurt one before they brought him down. He had to try, though. He had to do something.

He looked over the display panel. The digital touch screens made the system easy to figure out, and after a few seconds, Matan was able to discover that the Trident was not only armed, but it was equipped with missiles as well. His eyes swept across the sky and saw that a small reticule on the window followed his eyes movement. He grinned as he fixed his gaze on one of the Mothers. A second later, the reticule changed color from green to red.

"What are you doing?" Dr. Bach asked through the comm. "You disabled the autopilot."

"Fighting," Matan grunted and launched a missile at the Kaiju. The small missile struck the chest plate of the Mother, rocking her back on her heels. The Kaiju roared in pain, and as the smoke cleared, Matan could see a large hole in the Kaiju's chest. Bright orange blood poured from the wound. The Mother staggered and fell into the water, her body creating a large wave as she splashed down. "Killing Kaiju."

"I'm going to give you some help," Dr. Bach informed him. "You may feel a slight... tingling in your head, but it will pass."

A sudden pressure near the base of his skull nearly overwhelmed Matan. The Trident wobbled slightly as the pressure built and he was barely able to maintain a level flight. True to the doctor's word, though, it passed as quickly as it hit him and Matan found himself seeing everything around him in a manner he didn't think was possible. Multi-dimensional graphing overlaid his visual display and he could see varying ranges for different Mother Kaijus. He blinked and rubbed his eyes.

"Wow..." he breathed.

"You can now see what the drones I sent up to act as escorts can see," the doctor said. "Use them wisely."

Matan's feral grinned stretched nearly to his ears. He twisted the handle of the craft and took the Trident into a steep climb. The drones followed obediently after him. He leveled out and broke into a sharp turn. He directed the drones to focus their missiles on one Mother in particular, while he used the large cannons on the Trident to strafe the Kaiju, distracting her from the drones. Incendiary rounds exploded as they pierced her thick hide and the Mother howled in anguish as thousands of rounds impacted. She feebly swatted the air around her, but the drones, smaller than a grown man, easily slipped through her claws.

Two missiles lanced out from the drones and struck the Mother in her gaping maw. Blood, teeth and scales flew everywhere as the face of the Kaiju disappeared behind the twin explosions. Matan zipped past her as she began to totter, the damage extensive enough to throw the beast off-balance. Matan cackled madly and pushed the throttle forward for more speed. The Trident responded and he climbed back into the sky.

The drones warned him of the impending attack from another Mother. He dodged it with contemptuous ease and inverted the craft. He looked out the window and spotted the attacked. A large, bloated Mother covered in blisters was launching the small anti-aircraft Dragon Kaiju. Their silvery forms took to the sky, firing molten streams of metal at the drones as they zipped by. One lucky stream clipped a drone and Matan's vision wobbled as he lost the perspective of one of the drones.

The extra large Mother roared as two more drones launched their missiles at her. Matan followed their lead and fired three missiles of his own. The Dragons flew upwards to interpose their bodies in front of the target, their shapes obscuring the radar enough to cause two of the missiles to veer off and kill a Dragon instead of harming the Mother. Matan swore as the drones missed as well, their fiery warheads exploding harmlessly on the large Mother's well-armored back.

"Think you're clever, do you?" Matan growled as his cannons started firing, wiping out a dozen of the Dragons in one sweep of continuous fire. The aircraft shuddered as one Dragon clipped the wing of the Trident with its own. Matan regained control quickly and twisted the craft into a loop. The drones followed, though they were quickly falling to the Dragons. The plots he had moments before, so rich and detailed, were slowly disappearing under the assault of the Dragon Kaiju.

Matan watched one Mother Kaiju that appeared to be some sort of cross between a dragon and an ape take several drones to its chest, explosions blossoming over in showers of fire, shrapnel, and charred flesh that flew from the beast's body in smoking clumps. The Kaiju stumbled backwards, nearly falling, but managed to stay on its feet, despite the barrage. Another cluster of the drones flew across the air in front of its face, targeting its eyes with their guns. The thing howled in pain as the drones blinded it. It stumbled into the path of larger crab-like Mother Kaiju. The crab-like Kaiju angrily reached out with its pincers, drawing blood as they clasped the wounded Kaiju and flung it out of its path and into the murky water.

The wounded Kaiju rose back out of the water and let loose an earth-shattering roar of challenge. The crab-like Mother turned back and began to charge the wounded Kaiju. The two great beasts clashed, humanity forgotten as they vented their natural born rage and anger upon one another in a test of strength and might. Ignored, the drones continued to fire their guns into the two, wounding both and enraging them further. The combatants fell beneath the waves, pincers locked onto the throat of one Kaiju while teeth were embedded into the neck of the other.

Another Dragon flashed into view and he fired the cannons reflexively. The incendiary rounds tore the smaller Kaiju to pieces and he flew through the remains of it. Something small cracked the pane of glass, which protected him from the elements, the small crack quickly growing larger as the constant pressure from the winds escalated the problem. Matan slowed the Trident and the crack stopped growing, but now, he found himself with a new and unexpected problem.

A claw from a Mother Kaiju narrowly missed his Trident, and the acid stream she vomited up at him barely missed. The craft, moving just fast enough, managed to miss all of the corrosive liquid, but he knew that his time was running short. He had to give

Curri and the others a chance to get inside the bunker and do whatever Dr. Bach needed them to accomplish.

A plan began to form in the back of his mind, one so audacious and daring that he wasn't certain whether it was truly his idea or one implanted by the doctor.

"Dear God, please let this work," Matan whispered, praying for the first time since he had been a young boy being held in the protective arms of his mother, and before she had been ripped away during the Night of the Burning Sky. Before he had become a jaded and given up all hope for humanity's future. "Please."

The drones began to fly near the faces of the approaching Mother Kaiju, annoying them and buzzing close to their eyes and ears. The Mothers responded as he had hoped and they began to thrash wildly in the air. A Mother was accidently struck by another, and they howled at one another. The drones continued to instigate and prod them, angering them further. Matan fired another missile at them for good measure, and the two Mothers began to brawl, their single-minded purpose forgotten in their lust for blood and carnage.

The Trident shook violently. Matan glanced out the broken window and spotted a Dragon Kaiju clutching the wing of the aircraft. He tried to shake it off, but the Dragon held firm, the razor-sharp beak of the beast digging into the fuselage. He felt control of the aircraft slipping from his fingers and realized that his time was running out.

He took the Trident into a violent and steep dive, which caused the Dragon to lose its grip on the wing. However, the small Kaiju had managed to damage some of the electrical components within and the stabilizers were now shot. He could turn left and right still, but he could not take any sharp turns. His maneuverability had just been cut in half.

"Matan," Dr. Bach said over the comm. "You are doing good work, but I need you to do one more thing."

"Huh?" Matan asked as he began to pull out of his dive, or tried, at least. His hands were locked in position. He tried to move. No part of his body from his neck down was responding. Panic began to fill him. "Doctor, I can't move my arms!"

"I know."

"What do you mean?" Matan cried out.

"I need you to die in a blaze of glory," Dr. Bach said. "Curri's psychological profile that I've been able to build on her over the past few hours suggests that the loss of both you and the soldier named Higgins would give her the combined strength and despair she would need to activate the Verhys module."

"No... don't," Matan pleaded as tears began to form in the corner of his eyes. "I can do this. I can win."

"There is nothing to win, young man," Dr. Bach chided. "There is simply a task to accomplish and the means to facilitate it. You are nothing more than the means."

Matan began to swear and yell at the doctor as the Trident built up more speed. The propulsion kicked into overdrive and the aircraft screamed downward from the sky. Matan could see the dark blue water rushing up to meet him. He tried one last gambit.

"If you're going to kill me, drive me into one of those God-forsaken Mothers!"

Silence reigned over the comm for long, terrifying moments as the ocean grew bigger and bigger in his view. Matan's heart began to beat faster and faster before he felt his hand move, and pulled the stick back, taking him out of his dive. The g-forces pushed him back into the pilot's chair as he leveled out mere meters above the waves of the ocean. The Trident turned and lined up on another Mother Kaiju.

"Thank you," Matan whispered as missiles began to fly from the underbelly of the Trident. The Mother staggered from the onslaught and roared in pain. Matan felt the aircraft increase speed. "Thank you."

Matan felt another one of the Dragons land on the Trident's hull with a loud thud that shook the ship. The Trident wobbled as two more Dragons joined the first. Their claws tore and ripped at the ship's hull. Warning lights lit the entire console in front of him as the Dragons continued tearing into the ship. It no longer mattered – it was too late. The Trident crashed into the Mother Kaiju, turning itself and the Mother Kaiju's upper torso into a blazing eruption of burning fuel and detonating ordnance. Matan's last thought was of Curri. Her face flashed before his eyes as they were melted away inside their sockets.

The Mother Kaiju fell into the ocean, dead. Of the Trident or Matan, there was not a trace left.

****

Curri stared at the withered old man in the life support chair with unveiled disgust. Various tubes were connected to his frail body through the chair, and his sunken eyes were yellowed. Something in the chair hissed, a continuous sound that began to grate on the ragged edge of her nerves.

The room was quiet. The others in her tribe had elected to stay in another secure room together to be with one another when Curri activated the bomb. It left her alone, with the exception of the man on the video comm display who was looking down upon her. She turned away so she would not have to look at him as she tried to comprehend the massive device before her.

"What is your delay?" Dr. Bach asked over the comm. She glanced back at the horrible visage and realized that the device, which would probably end the world was far better to look at than the old man on the screen. It shocked her a little upon realizing this.

"Why didn't you just use one of your drones to activate the bomb?" she asked. "If it's so easy to activate, why didn't you just do it remotely?"

"Fail-safe reason," Dr. Bach replied with obviously thinning patience. "The designer implemented a DNA-sequencing lock on the scanner. Only a human can activate it, not a drone."

"Or a Kaiju," she muttered. Dr. Bach laughed. It was a wet, harsh sound.

"That would have been ironic," the doctor said. "Go over to the device and place your hand on the small screen on the left of the keypad." Curri followed his instructions. On the screen comm, Dr. Bach nodded weakly, his breathing in labored gasps. "Now type in the following numbers: 3–0–3. That should do it."

Curri obediently punched in the numbers. The machine buzzed and began to beep. "Now what?" She looked back at the comm screen. "Now what happens, Dr. Bach? *Dr. Bach?!*"

On the screen, the doctor was staring blankly at the screen, eyes unseeing. Behind him, Curri could just make out the signs of a machine struggling to keep the man as alive as it could. Something, and she wasn't sure what, had overtaxed the man's last bits of strength and energy. It rendered him unconscious, and probably put him into a coma. He would be of no more help to her, she figured. She looked away from the face of the wizened old man on the screen and back to the device. A small digital counter on the left of the DNA lock that she had activated was counting down. It took her a moment to translate the seconds counting down into something she recognized.

Three minutes. She had three minutes until the world ended by her hand.

Her mouth was dry. The bunker shook slightly as a Mother Kaiju outside began to strike the protective walls. Dust fell from the ceiling, as the shaking grew more concentrated. Curri stared at the device for a moment before she shifted her eyes to the doctor's slack face on the screen. Seeing no help there, she sat down on the floor and pressed her back against the wall. She stared numbly at the device as paneling began to fall from the ceiling, a not-so-subtle reminder of the Mother Kaiju who was above and trying to stomp a way into the bunker.

One minute left before the device fully activated, Curri's hands began to shake more as a deafening roar blasted through the bunker. She faintly heard the screams of the rest of her tribe as the Mother cracked open the walls of the bunker. The screams faded as the victorious howls of the Dog Kaiju filled her ears. She would have wept for them, but she had no more tears to shed. Not now, not ever.

The device activated. The floor beneath it disappeared as drills took it down into the Earth, accelerating to over ten times the speed of sound as it moved with single-minded purpose and determination. The resulting sonic boom ruptured her eardrums, and the flash from the propellant, which fueled the device, blinded her. She would have screamed in pain, but Curri's mind was completely and utterly broken. She sat there, deaf and blind, and waiting to die.

The device bore deeper into the Earth, driving for the core. Theoretical physics clashed with actual reality as the neutron bomb within the device triggered. The Veryhs module, which contained cold dark matter, a substance which had only been theorized about a mere twenty years before. The Veryhs module shook and began to break apart as the nanoseconds began to tick by, cold dark matter infusing the neutron bomb.

The neutron bomb, enhanced by the collapsing Veryhs module, created, for the briefest of instances, a small, dark matter fueled neutron star at the very heart of Earth's core. Pressure from the core immediately collapsed the star, causing what physicists call an "event horizon." Within this, a small space approximately fifteen meters wide disappeared from existence. Nanoseconds later, more of Earth's core disappeared as the black hole began to devour the planet from within.

Within two beats of Curri's heart, Earth ceased to exist.

End

 SEVEREDPRESS

f facebook.com/severedpress
twitter.com/severedpress

CHECK OUT OTHER GREAT KAIJU NOVELS

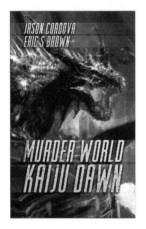

MURDER WORLD I KAIJU DAWN
by Jason Cordova
& Eric S Brown

Captain Vincente Huerta and the crew of the Fancy have been hired to retrieve a valuable item from a downed research vessel at the edge of the enemy's space.
It was going to be an easy payday.
But what Captain Huerta and the men, women and alien under his command didn't know was that they were being sent to the most dangerous planet in the galaxy.
Something large, ancient and most assuredly evil resides on the planet of Gorgon IV. Something so terrifying that man could barely fathom it with his puny mind. Captain Huerta must use every trick in the book, and possibly write an entirely new one, if he wants to escape Murder World.

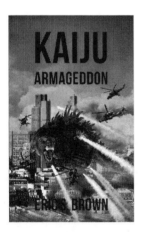

KAIJU ARMAGEDDON
by Eric S. Brown

The attacks began without warning. Civilian and Military vessels alike simply vanished upon the waves. Crypto-zool-ogist Jerry Bryson found himself swept up into the chaos as the world discovered that the legendary beasts known as Kaiju are very real. Armies of the great beasts arose from the oceans and burrowed their way free of the Earth to declare war upon mankind. Now Dr. Bryson may be the human race's last hope in stopping the Kaiju from bringing civilization to its knees.
This is not some far distant future. This is not some alien world. This is the Earth, here and now, as we know it today, faced with the greatest threat its ever known. The Kaiju Armageddon has begun.

 SEVEREDPRESS

f facebook.com/severedpress
twitter.com/severedpress

CHECK OUT OTHER GREAT KAIJU NOVELS

KAIJU WINTER
by Jake Bible

The Yellowstone super volcano has begun to erupt, sending North America into chaos and the rest of the world into panic. People are dangerous and desperate to escape the oncoming mega-eruption, knowing it will plunge the continent, and the world, into a perpetual ashen winter. But no matter how ready humanity is, nothing can prepare them for what comes out of the ash: Kaiju!

RAIJU
by K.H. Koehler

His home destroyed by a rampaging kaiju, Kevin Takahashi and his father relocate to New York City where Kevin hopes the nightmare is over. Soon after his arrival in the Big Apple, a new kaiju emerges. Qilin is so powerful that even the U.S. Military may be unable to contain or destroy the monster. But Kevin is more than a ragged refugee from the now defunct city of San Francisco. He's also a Keeper who can summon ancient, demonic god-beasts to do battle for him, and his creature to call is Raiju, the oldest of the ancient Kami. Kevin has only a short time to save the city of New York. Because Raiju and Qilin are about to clash, and after the dust settles, there may be no home left for any of them!

31511385R00031

Made in the USA
San Bernardino, CA
12 March 2016